PONY CAMP
diaries

Charlie and Charm

STRIPES PUBLISHING LIMITED
An imprint of the Little Tiger Group
1 Coda Studios, 189 Munster Road,
London SW6 6AW

A paperback original
First published in Great Britain by Stripes Publishing Limited in 2008
This edition published in 2019

ISBN: 978-1-78895-041-1

A CIP catalogue record for this book is available from the British Library.

Printed and bound in the UK.

10 9 8 7 6 5 4 3 2 1

PONY CAMP
diaries

Charlie and Charm

by Kelly McKain

Illustrated by Mandy Stanley

For Katie J, with thanks xx

THIS DIARY BELONGS TO

Charlie

Dear Riders,

A warm welcome to Sunnyside Stables!

Sunnyside is our home and for the next week it will be yours too! We're a big family – my husband Johnny and I have two children, Millie and James, plus two dogs ... and all the ponies, of course!

We have friendly yard staff and a very talented instructor, Sally, to help you get the most out of your week. If you have any worries or questions about anything at all, just ask. We're here to help, and we want your holiday to be as enjoyable as possible – so don't be shy!

As you know, you will have a pony to look after as your own for the week. Your pony can't wait to meet you and start having fun! During your stay, you'll be caring for your pony, improving your riding, enjoying long country hacks, learning new skills and making friends.

And this week's special activity is a day of fun at the beach with our ponies – just imagine cantering along the sandy shore together! Add swimming, games, a film night and a gymkhana and you're in for a fun-filled holiday to remember!

This special Pony Camp Diary is for you to fill with all your holiday memories. We hope you'll write all about your adventures here at Sunnyside Stables – because we know you're going to have lots!

Wishing you a wonderful time with us!

Jody xx

U Charlie and Charm U

Monday, after lunch

Well, here I am at Pony Camp, and Jody has given me this special diary to write all about it!

It's amazing here, with lots of ponies and two manèges and a swimming pool! And the girls are really lovely too. I just wish that Apple was here to enjoy it with me. She's my pony ... whoops, I mean she *was* my pony, but I got too big to ride her and Mum and Dad said they had to sell her. That was 1 month, 23 days and, erm, 5 hours ago. And I haven't ridden since – well, I hadn't until this morning anyway. I found it really strange being on a pony again and I was sad that it wasn't Apple.

When I got here there were other cars pulling up. Girls tumbled out, chattering excitedly and dragging big suitcases into the farmhouse.

I was feeling nervous, so I stayed close to Mum when she went to register me in the office. I wish I hadn't though, because she was doing that annoying thing of talking about me as if I'm not there, saying "Charlie" this and "she" that.

She was telling Sally the instructor and Lydia (one of the stable girls) about me not riding since they sold Apple. Well, actually she Apple said, "since we sold Apple" and I said, "since *you* did" because I had nothing to do with it – I would never have given up my lovely pony! Then she said how I won't even go back to the stables where I used to keep Apple on livery, and how I've lost touch with my riding friends because I always said no to going up there with them and after a while they stopped asking me.

I was getting really upset and annoyed, and

I think Sally noticed 'cos she sent me off into
the farmhouse to unpack and meet the other
girls. Lydia walked up there with me, and
on the way she squeezed my shoulders and
said, "Don't worry, Charlie, you'll be OK at
Sunnyside." That was so nice of her but it also
nearly made me start crying.

When I got to the room I started unpacking

straight away, to take my
mind off Apple. I could
hear girls chatting in the
other rooms but mine
was empty. The bed by

the window was unmade and covered in
clothes and mags, but the bunk beds looked
free, so I took the top one.

After a few minutes, Mum came up to
say goodbye because she had to get off to
work. She and Dad are always really busy at
their offices and my big bro Hughie is away

this week too, on an outward bound course in the Lake District. He loves canoeing over waterfalls and stuff like that. I used to be outdoorsy too – I practically lived at the stables while Apple was there! But when she was sold, I ended up moping around in my room not really knowing what to do with myself. Mum and Dad tried to talk to me about getting a new pony, but I was so upset I couldn't even think about it. In the end, Mum booked me on this holiday to try and cheer me up. That was only a couple of weeks ago and she kept saying how lucky I was to get the last place.

I tried to tell her that I didn't feel like riding, but she did that thing she does where she acts as if she's at work and bosses me about, saying things like, "Come on, darling, don't be silly

14

about this, it'll be good for you." Why can't she
just see that I miss Apple
so much it hurts? She
wasn't just a pony to
ride, she was my
best friend!

Best friends

I went down to
wave Mum off, and
when I got back upstairs
there was a girl sitting on the bottom
bunk cuddling a really tatty toy rabbit. When I
came in she stuffed it under her pillow, but
I got my frog Frieda out of my suitcase, where
I'd been hiding her.

The girl smiled and climbed up to sit on my
bunk, bringing her rabbit with her. "Have you
come on your own too?" she asked.

She was relieved when I said that I had.
She'd been worried that everyone would have
friends here already.

She's called Skye (and her rabbit is called Sniff) and she's nine, like me. She's from Wiltshire, which is kind of on the way back to London from here. She's got lovely long, dark hair with some little plaits and beads in, and she's wearing a really cool pink tie-dye top. When I asked where she got it from she said she'd dyed it herself! I'm going to try dying a couple of my T-shirts when I get home.

Then Millie, Jody's daughter, came bursting in (turns out she's the owner of the messy bed by the window!). She climbed up on

Me   Millie   Skye

my bunk too, and soon we were all chatting about what riding and stuff we'd done.

♘ Charlie and Charm ♘

When Millie told us she had her own pony
I ended up admitting that I used to have one.
I wasn't planning to tell anyone about Apple
in case I got upset, but it just came out. Skye
said she could imagine how I felt – poor thing,
her mum gave her cat away because of her
baby brother being allergic to it. And Millie said
how she couldn't even bear to imagine selling
her pony, Tally. I'm so relieved they don't think
I'm spoilt for being upset when I've been lucky
enough to have had my own pony in the first
place. It's great knowing they understand.

Jody came up and sent us
down to the yard then.
The other girls were
there and Sally and
Lydia, and we had
to go round in a circle
and say our names and
where we're from.

In the older girls' room there are:

Ricosha

Tameka

Jemima

Ricosha and Tameka are both 12 and they've come together from Croydon. Jemima is 11 and she's really giggly and cheeky, and she says she's always getting told off at school for talking in lessons!

The girls in the younger room are:

Yasmin

Ruby

Molly

Yasmin is from Hounslow, and Ruby and Molly have come together and live nearby. They're all eight.

Sally gave us these timetables so we can see roughly what we're doing each day, although she says it will change sometimes. In fact, it changed right away 'cos then we had a tour round the yard instead of a Pony Care lecture.

Pony Camp Schedule

8am: Wake up, get dressed, have breakfast
8.45am: Help on the yard, bring ponies in from the field, do feeds, etc.
9.30am: Prepare ponies for morning lessons (quick groom, tack up, etc.)
10am: Morning riding lesson
11am: Morning break - drink and biscuits
11.20am: Pony Care lecture
12.30pm: Lunch and free time
1.30pm: Prepare ponies for afternoon lesson
2pm: Riding lesson
3pm: Break - drink and biscuits
3.20pm: Afternoon Pony Care lecture
4.30pm: Jobs around the yard (i.e. cleaning tack, sweeping up, mixing evening feeds, turning out ponies)
5.30pm: Free time before dinner
6pm: Dinner (and clearing up!)
7pm: Evening activity
8.30pm: Showers and hot chocolate
9.30pm: Lights out and NO TALKING!

Sally showed us round Sunnyside and we all went *WOW!* when we saw the swimming pool and the games room. Then she took us into the main barn, where all the ponies that live out in the summer were waiting for us. Lydia was busy tacking them up ready for our lesson and the other girls got really excited, wondering which ponies they were going to get and saying how cute they looked.

The barn smelled exactly like the one on my old yard, and without thinking I began looking for Apple among the ponies. With a start I realized what I was doing. That barn smell made me miss her so much! I was

really relieved when we filed out again, to go to the fire drill meeting point.

Sally also went over some other safety things like:

1. How to tie a pony up properly.

2. How important it is to put all the equipment away and not leave things lying around.

3. How you must always tell someone where you're going if you leave the group, even if it's just to go to the loo or to get a different grooming brush from the tack room.

4. The correct boots and hats and body protectors, of course!

Then we all had to practise tying proper slip knots in our lead ropes. Molly got in a muddle, so I did hers, and then I did Ruby's too, because she was looking a little bit confused. I've tied up Apple so many times I can do it with my eyes closed, so it was no bother.

Then it was time to meet our ponies. We collected our hats, gloves and crops and went out on to the yard. Secretly, I felt really sick.

Sally said, "You'll each have your own pony for the whole week. You'll feed, groom and look after him or her as well as riding."

Everyone was grinning, and Ricosha and Tameka were actually jumping up and down with excitement, but I didn't feel that way at all. I didn't want a new pony to look after, even just for a week. I only wanted Apple.

It was great to see Skye so happy, though. She got a beautiful bay Arab cross called Fisher, with a lovely tumbling mane that's a bit like her own hair! They just seem to fit together, like me and Apple used to. Jemima got a palomino called Mischief, and she made us all laugh by saying, "Sounds like he'll suit

me! That's what Mum would say, anyway ...
and my teachers!"

Molly was so excited about getting Sugar
that it took ages to persuade her to stop
making a fuss of him and mount up!

I kept myself busy by helping out with the
other girls' stirrups, hoping that Sally wouldn't
notice me. But when I turned round she
was standing there with a grey Connemara.
"Charlie, meet Charm," she said, with a
smile. "He's a lovely boy and he'll definitely
cheer you up. Plus, he's a great
jumper." She winked at me and
added, "And you'll find out
why that matters later on."

Charm

I forced myself to smile back
and took the reins. I fussed over Charm
but only because Sally was watching. Inside,
I missed Apple so much I felt like crying. But
I took some deep breaths and managed

to hold the tears in – I don't want the girls thinking I'm a spoilt brat or something.

So, this is who everyone got in the end:

Me + Charm

Ricosha + Flame

Tameka + Shine

Millie + Tally

Ruby + Cracker

Skye + Fisher

Yasmin + Prince

Molly + Sugar

Jemima + Mischief (like her!)

I still didn't feel like riding, but I couldn't exactly say anything in front of everyone else, could I? So I got on, and it felt really strange because I was much higher up off the ground than I was on Apple. Also, Charm's slimmer than she was, so my legs were in a totally different position. I kept readjusting my stirrups, but I couldn't seem to find a leg position that felt quite right.

Still, even if I'm not really into the riding, the other girls are so nice I think I'll have a fun week. Like, it was so funny when Mischief wandered away from the mounting block, leaving Jemima hanging there giggling with her leg half over the saddle! We all laughed at

that, except Sally, of course, who said,
"Don't encourage him!" and made
him back up and stand properly
while Jemima got herself sorted out.

For our first lesson we all rode together
so that Sally could assess which group to
put us in. As we walked our ponies up to
the manège, the other girls kept saying how
gorgeous Charm was, but all I could think
about was Apple. I started getting upset, but
luckily Sally asked me to lead everyone into
the manège so I had to think about steering
Charm through the gate and on to the track.

It was so strange riding another pony after
Apple. As we trotted on,
Charm was going round with
his nose poking out (Apple
used to always get nicely on
the bit once we'd warmed up).
I shortened my reins to try and pull him in,

but that didn't seem to work. Sally called out,
"Relax your shoulders and get your elbows
back, Charlie. Charm's feeling your tension and
it's making him resist you."

I wanted to say, *It's not my fault he's not
paying attention to me.* But, of course, I didn't.
I just looked ahead and tried to relax more.
We made a few transitions from walk and trot
to halt, and Sally called out to all of us,
"I said forward to halt, which doesn't mean
just sitting there and letting your ponies run
out of steam!" Oh, dear! But at least I
wasn't the only one getting told off.

Then we did lots of changes of direction
and circles, and Sally got a few different people
to lead. That was easier for me because then
Charm could just follow the pony in front and
I didn't have to keep nagging at him. But when
it was my turn to trot a 20 metre circle I had
to use my legs loads to even get him off the

track! And when we cantered to the back of
the ride (you could choose if you wanted to
or not) it took me two corners to get a canter.
That was a shock – I only ever had to sit down
and touch Apple with my outside leg and she'd
whoosh straight off.

At lunchtime I sat with my two room-mates,
and Millie told us what it's like living at the
stables all the time. It sounds amazing! I wish I
lived somewhere like this – if I did there would
have been plenty of space to keep Apple and
she could have stayed with me for ever.

When we were helping clear up after lunch, Ricosha and Tameka showed us this singing and dancing routine they've been working on. Me, Millie, Skye and Jemima tried to learn a bit of it. We weren't exactly very good and we all kept bursting into giggles! It was so much fun and it felt like being back with the girls at my old stable yard before I stopped going. It made me really miss them.

Then Sally came in and read out the groups, and would you believe this is the exact thing she said?

Charlie, I've put you in Group B because of all your experience, but you need to stay focused and pay attention or I might decide to move you to Group A where you can have more opportunity to focus on your partnership with Charm.

I was just *staring* at her then, probably
with my mouth hanging wide open.
I couldn't believe it, I'd nearly
ended up in the *beginners'* group!
Me and Apple used to ride in the
advanced lessons at my stables!
I couldn't help feeling annoyed with Charm
for not listening to me. He really made me look
bad in the assessment!

It's strange that he's being so naughty when
Sally keeps saying how great he is. Oh! I've just
had a secret thought. What if it's just that he
doesn't like *me*?

On my bunk bed after dinner, chilling out!

This afternoon we had our first Pony Care lecture, which was all about tack, and Lydia showed us how to tack up on Yasmin's cute piebald, Prince. I knew how, 'cos of Apple, but the younger ones hadn't ever done it on their own, and even Jemima wasn't sure about whether the noseband did up under or over the cheek pieces. Lydia explained about some of the different bits and nosebands and what they're for, which was interesting 'cos I only ever rode Apple in a cavesson and Eggbutt snaffle. Then she pointed to parts of the saddle and we had to call out what they were. They are:

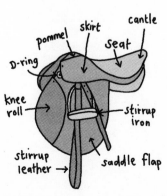

Then we had to try tacking up for ourselves.
I helped Jemima check Mischief's saddle when
she wasn't sure if it was in the right place, then
I put the bits in for Ruby and Molly because
they hadn't done it before and I was worried
they might trap their fingers. I was about to help
Skye pick out Fisher's feet (in case he trod on
her toes) when Lydia came over to me and said
I needed to get on with tacking up Charm or
we wouldn't be ready in time for the lesson.
I told her it was fine 'cos I'm quick at it, but she
said, "I didn't really mean that, Charlie. It's about
spending time with your pony. You can
always give him a good brush as well."
So I tacked Charm up in about two
minutes, because he didn't look like he needed a
brush first to me. I didn't know what to do after
that, so I just fiddled about with my boot
until everyone was ready, pretending
that I'd got a stone down it.

◡ Charlie and Charm ◡

After the lesson this afternoon, I definitely
think I'm right about Charm not liking me!
It's not that he bucked me off or anything,
but he didn't even try to do things properly.
I just couldn't seem to get any impulsion, so
I had to flap around to make a transition,
and he kept trying to put his head down and
yank the reins out of my hands, as though
he didn't want me riding him. Sally told me
to relax again and a couple of times she got
annoyed because my mind wandered off and
I didn't hear her instructions. Of course, it
was because I was thinking of Apple and how
much fun we'd be having if she'd come on
this holiday with me.

Mischief was being
cheeky in the lesson,
cutting off the corners,
and Sally said Jemima had
to stop finding it funny and

Silly Mischief!

concentrate on keeping her inside leg on, so at least I wasn't the only one having problems.

There was one good thing, though – quite an exciting thing, actually! After the lesson, Sally called us all into the middle and announced that she'll be taking a few of us out on to the cross-country course! That was the special surprise Jody mentioned in her welcome letter! Sally also told us we'll be having a mini cross-country competition on Friday when all the parents are here!

I've always wanted to try cross country, ever since our stables went on this day trip to the Burghley Horse Trials.

It was totally amazing watching the horses leap over these giant fences right in front of you! I've taken Apple over

the odd log or low hedge on a hack out and
even that was really exciting, so I can't wait!

After Sally had made the announcement,
she smiled at me and added, "That's
why I said you're lucky you've
got Charm, Charlie, because
he's such a great jumper!"

I made myself smile back, but
all I could think of was how much
Apple would've loved jumping a whole course
and how we never got the chance to try it.

Skye was really unsure about having a go
and Sally promised her that no one has to
do anything they don't want to here at Pony
Camp. "It's no problem if you want to join
in with Group A while we go out on the
course," she told her, then said to us all, "And
if I don't feel that some of you are ready to
tackle cross country, I'll ask you to join the
other group."

Ricosha and Tameka gave each other a worried look then, because they weren't sure Sally would think they were ready. She's going to decide who's allowed to do it after tomorrow morning's lesson and I really hope she will let them join in. It'll be way more fun if we can all do it together.

Oh, gotta go now. Ricosha's saying that today's dryer-uppers have finished (we've got a rota – I'm on it with Skye on Wednesday), and Millie and Skye have just come in to change 'cos we're all going swimming!

I'm snuggled up in bed
with Frieda - writing this
by the light of my torch!

Swimming was really fun and so was running
back through the house in our towels, doing
giant leaps so as not to make too
many wet footprints. Then we
had showers and Jody helped us
dry our hair and made us all hot
chocolate in the kitchen.

Millie and Skye are both asleep
now, but we were all whispering
for ages after lights out. Skye is still
worried about doing the cross country and
Millie was trying to tell her how great she did
in the lesson this afternoon. I said something
about how Skye shouldn't worry because
she'll easily manage the course, and suddenly
everything seemed to go wrong.

"Well, I'm sorry I'm not as confident as you, Charlie!" she said in a grumbly voice, and then got up and marched off to the loo.

"Well done, Charlie," Millie whispered.

"What did I say?" I hissed. "I only meant she's a really good rider."

"Well, you said, 'don't be so silly, it's easy-peasy!' like she's stupid for worrying."

My stomach flipped over and I felt my face go burning hot. Had I really said that? "I didn't mean it that way," I insisted.

When Skye came back I said sorry about my words coming out wrong, and how I'd only meant it like she's a really good rider.

Luckily, she was OK about it – phew! She's still not sure about doing the cross country, but she's going to think about it at least.

Goodnight!

Tuesday, I'm quickly writing this before we get called down for lunch

Well, now I know for sure that Charm doesn't like me.

In our lesson we were working on the skills we'll need for the cross country. Me and Charm started off OK-ish, but when we were all practising our jumping position down the long side he took advantage of me not having as much control as usual and kept veering off the track on purpose. I was trying really hard but he just wouldn't listen to me.

Sally didn't see it like that though. I wish she didn't think Charm was so perfect, then she might stop blaming me for his mistakes. She called out, "Charlie, the more annoyed you get the less Charm is going to co-operate with you because he senses your tension. Breathe out, sit deep in the saddle and relax your arms and shoulders."

I did it but I felt embarrassed with everyone watching.

"That's better," she said. "Now, start again." I tried to stay relaxed, but I still felt upset after the lesson. Maybe that's why an awful thing happened in the Pony Care lecture. Something else came out of my mouth all wrong, like it did to Skye last night. Only this time it was to Jemima.

I wasn't going to write this down but I can't seem to get it out of my head. We were learning about grooming, standing in the barn with our ponies, copying what Lydia was showing us on Shine. As we were doing circles with our rubber curry combs, she said something like, "A good partnership in the manège or on the cross-country course starts right here, girls. Spending time with your pony, talking to him or her, grooming and caring, all lay the foundations for your partnership while riding."

Before she said that I'd thought I was just brushing a pony, but then suddenly it felt like I was being disloyal to Apple. Jemima was next to me and she was cooing all over Mischief, telling him how gorgeous he was while she gently wiped his eyes with the special blue sponges in his grooming kit. I tried to ignore it, but she kept going on and on and on.

Then I started imagining Apple having her eyes wiped by Laura, her new owner, and I wondered if she's completely forgotten about me already. That made me feel really upset and that's when Jemima said, "Charlie, can I borrow your curry comb when you've finished? Mischief's seems to be missing from his kit."

Before I could stop myself, I snapped, "No, you can't!"

Jemima just blinked at me in shock, her usual cheeky grin gone. I could feel my cheeks burning with embarrassment. I still can't believe I said that!

I didn't know what to do then, so I went round the other side of Charm where Jemima couldn't see me. After the lecture, I wanted to say sorry to her, but she walked off really fast, arm in arm with Skye, and now she won't catch my eye.

Oh dear! Things just don't seem to be going very well for me at all.

At least I've got the cross country to look forward to. We're walking the course tomorrow, and then going out on our ponies for a practice. I'm really keen to see what jumps we'll be doing and how high they are.

Gotta go – Jody's calling that lunch is ready.

I can't believe what just happened!

My hand's shaking so much I can hardly write. Sally hasn't chosen me to do the cross country!

And worse still, everyone else in our group is doing it!

I feel so silly. I just assumed I'd be taking part, and instead I'll have to go in with the beginners tomorrow. I don't understand. I'm about the most experienced rider here, with Millie and Jemima, anyway. I can easily manage a few cross-country fences!

Sally came in just when we were finishing lunch and made the announcement. I was sure there'd been a mistake, so I hurried out after her. "Did you just say I'm not doing the cross country?" I asked.

"Yes," she said, and carried on walking.

"But why?" I gasped.

"Because I'm the instructor and I don't think you're ready," she told me, still walking.

But I wouldn't give up. "Skye's allowed, and she's not that experienced or confident!"

Sally sighed and said, "You haven't been putting the effort in, Charlie. You're not focused enough."

"But I'm one of the best riders here," I argued.

"It's not just about technical ability," she said. "Riding's about being a team with your pony. Cross country can be dangerous and you need to have a good partnership."

Huh! How unfair is that?!

"But that's *Charm's* fault," I insisted. "He doesn't listen to me. He'd be better in a flash or drop noseband and a stronger bit..."

Sally stopped in her tracks and looked

44

me straight in the eye. I suddenly realized I was talking back to an instructor and I felt a bit scared. "Charlie, the problem is not your pony," she said sharply. "I know Charm. He's got a lovely nature and he's very well mannered."

"But..." I began.

"Charlie," she said again, cutting me off. "The problem is you."

I stood there feeling stunned as she marched into the office. Why doesn't she understand? Can't she see what Charm is really like?

So that's why I've been hiding round the back of the feed barn ever since, writing this and trying not to cry.

I wish I could just go home.

Oh no, Millie's calling me. I suppose I'd better get back to the yard.

We've just finished on the yard - I've found a little space in the tack room to sit and write in here

Oh dear! This afternoon didn't go very well either. In fact, everything seems to be going more and more wrong for me!

I was too embarrassed to look at Sally after what happened at lunchtime, and I was so annoyed with Charm for making me miss out on the cross country that I felt really tense and I couldn't seem to control him at all.

ME
Seesawing!

He wouldn't go into canter, so I started see-sawing back and forth to try and make him. Sally called out, "You're tensing up as you go into the corner and letting his nose poke out, Charlie. He's not collected, he's got no impulsion. Shorten up your reins, sit deep into your saddle, relax your arms and keep your leg on rather than kicking like that!" She said it in a fed-up way like it was the millionth time she'd told me. I did try, but it just didn't work. I mean, I know how I should do it – it's not my fault Charm ignores me!

Mischief was playing up too, but after a few times when he cut off the corner, Jemima got him into a lovely canter. I was so busy feeling cross about Charm's behaviour that by the time I realized everyone was cheering for Jemima they'd stopped. Then Sally made it worse by saying, "Please don't sulk, Charlie, you can do as well as that if you put your mind to it." So then everyone thought I hadn't cheered on purpose! They all looked at me and I got completely red and flustery.

Then in the Pony Care lecture on feeding it was awful 'cos we had to get into pairs – Ricosha and Tameka went together, and Millie and Yasmin, and Ruby and Molly, and Skye and Jemima, and I was left with no one. Lydia said, "Charlie, just make a three, that's fine," but as

I looked around no one smiled at me or invited me to join up with them. I went with Millie and Yasmin in the end,

but I don't think Yas exactly wanted me there.

We had to make up feeds for horses who do different amounts of work, and Yas didn't seem to have any ideas, even though Millie tried to help her think. Then Jody called Millie in to do her maths practice. Yas still wasn't saying anything, and in the end we got so behind the others that I just had to fill in the whole sheet myself.

I'd better go in now, before I get into trouble for not telling anyone where I am.

Still Tuesday

It's 11.34pm, but I'm still awake because I've been having a whispery chat with Millie. I was crying loads, so she came to sit on my bunk and we ended up talking for ages. I'm so upset because, well, to explain it properly I'll have to start from the beginning.

This evening we all went outside to play games like limbo and stuck in the mud. It was really fun, but when Jemima and Tameka were picking teams for the volleyball I ended up being picked last and just standing there on my own. There were four on each team and Jemima said, "It's OK, you lot can have Charlie," so I went on Tam's team.

I thought Jemima only said that to be nice to the other team. But then afterwards, when we were going inside, I went to put the

coloured bands back into the games room,
and when I came out I saw Jemima and Skye
huddled together in the passageway.

Jemima whispered, "I so didn't
want Charlie on our team. She's
such a spoilt brat. I can't believe
she wouldn't even lend me her
curry comb, or say well done
when I finally got Mischief round
that corner. And Yas says she was too scared
of her to suggest anything when they were
doing the feeds thing! And she totally took over
when Molly and Ruby were tacking up!"

I ducked back behind the door, my stomach
churning – why didn't they realize I was only
trying to help the younger girls? And I only did
all the feed questions myself because Yasmin
didn't have any ideas! I hoped Skye would stick
up for me, but then I heard her say, "She was
mean to me too, about the cross country."

I nearly leaped out and cried, "But I said sorry and you said it was OK!" but I made myself stay where I was. My heart was hammering so hard I felt sure they'd hear it.

"She's a nightmare!" Jemima said then. "I mean, if she doesn't want to be here why did she come? She's spoiling it for everyone else!"

As they walked off, I stayed frozen to the spot, my legs trembling. I felt really sick hearing them talk about me like that.

Because suddenly I saw everything differently.

And I knew they were right.

I hung around in the games room by myself for ages, and then Jody came and sent me upstairs, saying it was almost time for lights out. I got ready quickly and jumped into bed before anyone could say anything. Skye was already asleep, even though the light was still on. Jody said goodnight and once it was dark I tried to go to sleep as well, but I couldn't stop thinking about what they'd said. The tears I'd been bottling up inside since I got here just started pouring out and I couldn't stop them.

That's when Millie crept up to my bunk.

I was all sniffly and I kept bursting into more tears, but I managed to tell her what Jemima and Skye had said about me.

Millie just put her arm
round me and nodded,
and she didn't look like she
hated me or anything.

"I've been so wrapped
up in my own feelings about Apple, it seems
like I've been really horrible to people," I said
then. "But I haven't meant to be – honestly."

Millie didn't have a massive go at me, but
instead just said, "Don't worry. It'll blow over."

"It won't!" I sobbed. "I don't even blame
them for not liking me. And Sally was right –
I haven't even given Charm a chance! I haven't
bothered to get to know him at all, or to
spend any time with him."

Millie squeezed my shoulders and said,
"Well, turning your thinking round is the first
step to making changes! That's what Mum
always says, anyway. Now you've done that
everything should get easier."

I can't believe Millie was still nice to me after how I've acted. She really is a cool girl. I know I've lost my chance to do the cross country, but at least I can still enjoy my week here, starting tomorrow. I'll be extra specially friendly to the girls and I'm going to try really, really hard with Charm.

Wednesday, it's nearly time to go down to the yard -
and I've got butterflies in my tummy!

I'll tell you why in a minute!

Today is my brand-new start at Pony Camp and it's been going quite well so far. At breakfast, when Yasmin was telling us about her riding stables I listened to her properly without any interrupting. I think she was a bit surprised but she seems happier to chat to me now, so that's good.

Then when it was clearing up and brushing teeth time, Jody wanted someone to take the staff rota to Sally, and I offered to do it. I wanted to talk to her on my own, even though my heart was pounding in case she got cross with me again. As I handed her the rota, I said sorry for not giving Charm a chance and I promised to try harder in her lessons.

She smiled. "Good girl, Charlie," she said. "And remember, enjoying Charm doesn't mean you're letting Apple down."

I hadn't realized it, but that's how I've been feeling, like if I have a good time with Charm then I'm being mean to Apple. I sat down on the bench in the office, because suddenly my legs felt very wobbly. Sally sat next to me and put her arm round my shoulders. "Apple will always be with you in your heart and in your happy memories, but she wouldn't want you to stop riding, would she?" she said gently.

I couldn't say anything back because my throat felt all funny, but I managed to shake my head.

Then Sally said something amazing that I wasn't expecting at all, which was, "I don't usually go back on my decisions, but this is a special case. Ride well this morning and I'll think about letting you do the cross country after all."

How brilliant is that?!

That's why I've got butterflies!

I'm going to work so hard with Charm in the lesson and fingers crossed Sally will let us do the course.

I had a chance to say sorry to Charm too, because this morning during yard duties, Sally said he looked a bit muddy and asked me to give him a good groom. I spent ages cleaning his face and combing his mane, while telling him all about Apple and how much I've been missing her.

"I'm so sorry for not making friends with you before," I told him. He nudged my arm and gave me a look, as if he understood. Then I explained we still had a chance to do the cross country. He seemed excited, and it's good that by spending time together we've started to become friends.

We're having our Pony Care lecture now, which is called 'All About Ponies', on markings and breeds and conformation. If we do anything in twos I hope someone wants to go with me today. I'm going to just smile and be really nice, so hopefully they will!

fingers crossed!

Just quickly writing this before lunch

Johnny called Sally away straight after the lesson because someone was on the phone, so I don't know if I can do the cross country yet. The lesson went quite well, but me and Charm didn't get everything right, so I'm not sure if Sally will say yes. Argh! I'm so nervous, waiting to hear! I know – I'll write in here about the rest of the morning to try and take my mind off the suspense.

Me and Charm are even friendlier now. He's definitely beginning to like me (and he loves me ruffling his mane up!). I like him too – he's got lovely dark eyes, which make it look like he's thinking important thoughts.

Things are going a bit better with the other girls too. When we were grooming and tacking up I helped Molly to pick out Sugar's feet, because she was a bit nervous of him standing on her toes. But instead of taking over, I showed her how to lean into him a bit and run her hand down his leg until he picked his hoof up. She was so proud when she did it all by herself. I'm not sure if Jemima saw. I really hope she did. Then she might stop thinking I'm a spoilt brat, and Ricosha and Tameka might be friendly to me again too, because they tend to do what Jemima does and right now they are kind of half not talking to me.

In our Pony Care lecture we had to go round the yard in twos writing down the different markings on the ponies and guessing which breeds they might have in them. Millie wasn't there because she's done all this before, and as soon as Lydia said get into pairs Jemima grabbed Skye's hand. I tried not to mind and made myself keep smiling, and I was surprised (and v. happy) when Molly said she wanted to go with me. When it was her turn with the clipboard I spelled out some words for her, but only when she asked me to.

In the lesson (my big test!), we warmed up in walk and trot on each rein and did lots of turns and circles to get our ponies listening. We worked on getting a collected, controlled canter with lots of impulsion for the cross country. It's not as if Charm and I were doing everything perfectly, but we were definitely more of a team. Sally set up three jumps and we worked over them, trying to look ahead at the next one as we landed.

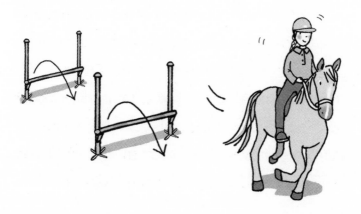

Sally kept calling out, "Look ahead and think ahead!" to everyone, which is her motto. (She's also always saying that we have to make sure we give our ponies the freedom of their head and necks as we go over the jumps.) I tried not to wonder what Sally was thinking of my riding. Instead, I just focused on working with Charm. Jemima got Mischief over the jumps after a couple of run outs and everyone said well done. I said it the loudest and she smiled at me and my stomach flipped over and I started thinking that maybe everything will turn out OK after all. Oh, Sally's...

*　　*　　*

Yes, I can do the cross country! Yesssssssss!!! Sally said I had really tried and shown good improvement, although I've still got things to work on. Gotta go to lunch now. But I just want to quickly write again that I AM DOING THE CROSS COUNTRY – HOORAY!

The cross-country practice was amazing!!

I'm going to put down everything I did, but first I need to go back to where I left off and write about this afternoon so I don't miss anything out.

After lunch, instead of having a Pony Care lecture, our group went out with Sally and walked the cross-country course! Most of us had never done proper cross country before. We didn't have to decide our own route in and out of each jump, thank goodness! Instead, Sally showed us the best lines of approach. She also helped us line up the jumps with objects in the distance so we could make sure we were on the right track.

We were all really excited, but also a bit scared because the jumps look so solid we were worried they'd hurt our ponies' legs if we didn't get over cleanly. Sally explained that fixed jumps are actually less scary to ponies because they can see them more easily. That means they tend to judge the take-off better and do a bigger jump (as I soon found out on Charm!). Luckily, the ground's pretty much flat so we don't have to worry about going up or downhill either – phew!

Skye walked the course with us but she still wasn't sure about having a go. In the end she decided to try a few of the jumps with us today, and then think about whether to do the whole course and the competition after that.

Here is my pic of the course. I've written some of the helpful hints Sally gave us on it, so I can remember what she said.

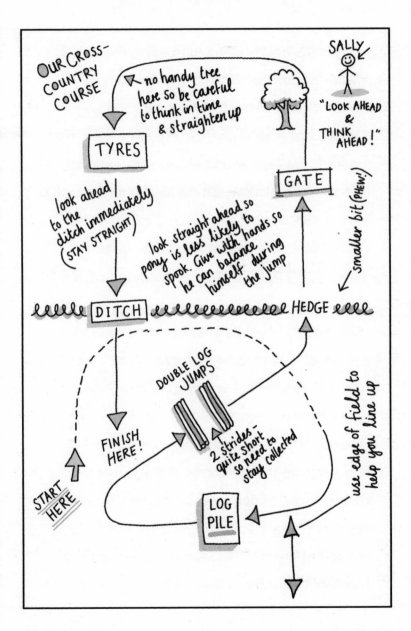

We were all buzzing with excitement as we went back to the yard to tack up our ponies ready for the cross-country practice. I was telling Charm all about the course while I did up his throatlash and made sure his numnah was straight underneath his saddle. Of course, I know he couldn't understand exactly what I was saying, but he could tell we were in for some **FUN!** His ears pricked up and he started wandering out of the barn before I'd even got the reins over his head to lead him!

We all mounted in the yard, then rode into the manège to warm up. Charm's trot was bouncier than usual and his canter was quicker off the leg. I think it was because I was listening to him more, so I knew when he needed a nudge, plus I had a much more relaxed contact so he wanted to work with me in the first place. I was surprised at how much better things were – I think I'm starting to see why Charm is called Charm. Sally gave me a wink and a smile – she'd noticed the improvement too! When she led us out of the manège and up to the field my heart was thumping with excitement.

To start with, we all had a turn of going over the log, past the double and back over the log again, just to get used to jumping out in the open. Skye was a bit nervous at first, and Fisher lost confidence and ran out on their first try. When she got over on the second go, we all cheered, and Sally said, "See? It's as easy as jumping over a log – ha ha!"

Next we had a go at the log and the double! Sally warned us that we had to keep collected over the two brush fences as the strides in between are quite short. Mischief rushed it and only put in one stride, and then he had to take a giant leap to get over the second half of the fence. We all gasped and

squeezed our eyes shut but they made it over
– just! Sally told Jemima to circle him a couple
of times to get a more collected canter and
then bring him round again, and this time
Jemima had more control and he got the two
strides in.

When it was my go I was thinking about
what strides Charm was doing and when I
should go into the jumping position, and I
bobbed up too early. I had to grab on
to his mane so I didn't go flying
over his head! Sally told me to
let the pony do the jumping and
to "look ahead and think ahead".
We were all smiling at each
other when she said it. I tried
again but I still got my timing wrong.

Then we all jumped the hedge into the
next field (which was really fun because it
was so soft we weren't panicking about our

ponies' hooves brushing it!). Charm loved it
and so did I. We flew over and
as we came to a halt I
gave him a big pat to say
well done.

Great job!

In the next field we
jumped the gate and the
spread fence, but we didn't add the ditch on.
Sally said we'd tackle that on Friday morning
as she didn't want us to do too much all at
once. Even Skye enjoyed herself in the end
and she couldn't stop grinning when we were
riding back to the yard. I really think she might
do the competition after all!

When we got back to the barn I grabbed
a quick drink from the fountain and took my
very hot hat off! Then I untacked Charm and
spent loads of time fussing him and telling him
how well he'd done. He seemed really proud
of himself, and as he nuzzled my arm with his

soft muzzle I thought he was trying to let me know that he was proud of me too – not just for the cross country, but for cheering up and trying hard.

I wish we could have another practice on the course tomorrow but we've got our day trip out to the beach instead. That will be loads of fun, though, and I'm totally looking forward to cantering on the sand with Charm. I just wish we had more time to work on our cross-country skills as well!

And we certainly need it – back in the yard, Sally gave us all helpful comments on our weak areas. I can't remember everything, but Jemima's was to keep control of Mischief's pace with half halts and by changing down into trot when he's getting too strong in canter.

Ricosha's was to ride Flame more positively towards the jump so that she has less chance of refusing, and to look over to the other side of the jump rather than at it.

It was so funny when Sally turned to Millie because Millie knew exactly what she was going to say – "Keep Tally on course." He needs to stay focused after each jump because he likes to tear off randomly across the field!

Then it was my turn. Sally said that I wasn't quite trusting Charm to clear the jump, how I was looking down instead of ahead sometimes and also going into the jumping position too early. She called it getting in front of the pony, which she says is a bad idea because it's very easy to come flying off that way! I've really got some catching up to do, but I'm glad I'm not the only one with things to work on.

She also said I need to concentrate on leading Charm instead of trying to do the jump for him. I knew what she meant, but it still made me giggle, imagining this!

When she'd given us all our comments, she said, "And one final thing for all of you to remember..." and we chanted, "Look ahead and think ahead!" and then burst into giggles! Sally grinned and said, "You're a cheeky bunch, but at least you're listening, I suppose!"

I couldn't help grinning too. It's so great to be one of the cheeky bunch again!

In bed

I've tried going to sleep (like Millie and Skye)
but I'm too excited about everything! So I've
put my torch on and I'm writing this
under the covers instead.

Tonight, after Skye and I had done our
drying-up duty, we had another games
evening ... but in the swimming pool this time!
It was so funny – we had these relay races
where you do different strokes, and then
hopping and jogging, passing a float, throwing
a ball to the next person and things like that.

Jody put us into teams and when she
said, "Charlie, you're with Skye, Jemima and
Yasmin," it was really cool because Skye went,
"Yes!" like she was really happy they were
getting me, and Jemima smiled at me as well.
Millie's brother James joined in to even out
the numbers and Ricosha and Tameka kept

giggling about having a boy on their team.
That was cool because it put them off a bit
and we won the first two races! Hee hee!
Then they won two and then it was the

final race —
the tiebreaker.
When the
last person in

each team was on the way back we all started
cheering madly. Molly was our last one, jogging
through the water with the float, and we all
cheered her on, and guess what... We won!
Jody said it was because we'd worked really
well as a team. I just hope I can make a good
team with Charm too, so we trust each other
more in the cross country. If we can do that I
still think we might have a chance to win.

I've got to put this diary down now, 'cos
my eyes are closing on their own...

☾ Charlie and Charm ☾

Thursday, after tea

We had such a great time at the beach today! Before we left we had our Pony Care lecture about bandages for travelling. Lydia did a demo on Shine, then we all had a go on our ponies' legs and tails. It was quite hard to get the tail bandage right – when Lydia inspected them we were all laughing 'cos she only just touched Molly's and it fell off Sugar's tail, and mine wasn't much better either!

We didn't have space in the horse box to take all the ponies to the beach, so we had to double up and share. Sally brought her own horse, Blue, and she let Jemima ride him too! Skye and me rode Charm (yay!), Ricosha and Tameka shared Flame, Millie and Yasmin rode Prince, and Ruby and Molly rode Sugar.

I let Skye ride first and she kept to the sand because Charm wasn't too keen on the water.

But when it was my turn, with Sally helping me, I got him into the foamy waves. She told me to ride him forward and act like everything was fine, and after a couple of little panics he decided it must be OK if I thought so!

Soon we were playing that game where you wait for the waves, and then turn around and try to race away from them. I always play it with Hughie on holiday in Cornwall but it was loads more fun on horseback. Charm loved it too! He shook his head in delight as this one big wave crashed round his legs, and he looked so cute I just had to lean forward and give him a big hug!

After that, me, Millie and Tameka had a canter up the beach with Sally, and she showed us how to get lots of impulsion without getting the ponies too excited. I think I've finally got the hang of half halts now and how to squeeze Charm forward with my leg so he has more energy in the canter instead of just getting faster. He's certainly not going along with his nose poking out any more!

Later on, Sally found these two bits of driftwood and set them up as jumps. Flame wouldn't take Tameka over on her own, so Sally gave her a lead and they went flying over! Then we all wanted to try giving leads, so we kept going over in pairs in different combinations. I went with Millie, then with Tam, then Sally, and afterwards I just couldn't stop grinning! Then we swapped round and Jemima, Skye and Ricosha had a few goes over the jumps too, and we all cheered for them.

The trip was so brilliant I didn't want it to end! On the minibus home we were all singing songs and giggling about girly stuff, like Jemima liking this boy in her village. Sally came and chatted to us too, and when everyone else was busy singing, she asked how I was.

That's when I realized I'd been so caught up in the fun I'd hardly missed Apple all day. And I said, "I feel great! I wanted to practise on the cross-country course today, but it's actually lucky that we came to the beach, because I got the chance to get Charm to trust me about splashing in the waves and I know how to get a collected canter now and he jumped that driftwood even better than the logs on the course!"

Sally did a mysterious kind of smile and said, "Yeah, lucky that. I hadn't planned it at all!" and I knew she meant that she had! She's such an amazing teacher and so is Charm. We're really turning into a team now!

Oh, gotta go, it's time for our film night (with popcorn – yum!). We're going to watch this one about the Burghley Horse Trials and get some inspiration for the cross-country comp tomorrow!

Friday morning, and I've just woken up

It's cross-country day – hooray!! But also our last day at Pony Camp – boo!!

The film we saw last night was amazing. The fences were HUGE! We were all going "oooh!" and "ahhhh!" watching the horses and riders go over them, and "eeeeeekkkk!" and "wow!" when they were jumping the really tricky ones like the coffin. We're even more excited about getting out on to the cross-country course after seeing that!

Skye, Millie and me had planned to stay up and have a midnight feast because it was our last night here (well, mine and Skye's anyway), but we all fell asleep by accident! I've just remembered I had a really weird dream about Apple. We were on a beach and I was cantering

Zzzzzz

along on her, and then suddenly I was on Charm instead and Apple was standing with Laura, the girl who bought her. Somehow I just knew Apple was happy, and I felt happy for her. When I woke up I still felt that way too!

Of course I'll always miss Apple, but I'm sure she's having fun with Laura, and I suppose it is nicer to have an owner the right size to ride you, so that you can have lots of adventures together.

I've got to get dressed now because we're having another lesson on the cross-country course this morning, and then getting our ponies ready for the comp!

I can't wait!!!

♡ Charlie and Charm ♡

Still Friday!

I'm back at home, I've had a shower and I'm
in my pyjamas – Mum couldn't believe it when
I said I wanted to go to bed early! Really I
wanted to come up to my room and finish
off my Pony Camp diary before I forget one
single thing about my amazing day!

For our morning lesson we warmed up in
the manège and then went out to practise on
the cross-country course. Sally asked me to
give Skye a lead over the log to get
her started on a good note. I was
so proud that she'd chosen me
and Charm to lead someone
else over a jump! And I could
tell that Charm was pleased
with himself too! After jumping in pairs on the
beach yesterday we just flew over, and Skye
and Fisher followed on with no worries.

Everyone was much less nervous and giggly than the first time we came out on to the course, probably because the beach ride had given us more confidence. Plus, it wasn't as hot today, so we weren't so absolutely boiling in our body protectors and long sleeves and hats and everything! We did the course in two parts – first we had a go at the log pile, the double and the hedge, and then when we were all over in the next field we tried the gate, tyre jump and...

Yes, we finally tackled the ditch!

The water looked a bit **SPOOKY!** because the bank either side was really grassy and there were bushes hanging over it, which made strange reflections. But after getting Charm into the waves, I knew that he would trust me around spooky-looking water, as long as I acted like it was fine. In fact, I stayed so calm and confident, and Charm was so into his stride after the tyre jump that he didn't even think about standing off at the ditch and just popped straight over it!

Once Skye had seen us clearing it, she decided to have a go too. It was a bit messy, with Fisher putting the brakes on and then doing a massive leap so she had to cling on, but at least they got over! Sally said, "Well, now you've done the ditch and both halves of the course, you might as well go in for the competition this afternoon. But, of course, you don't have to if you don't feel like it..."

"I'd like to," Skye said shyly and we all gave her a cheer. "But I'm telling you now I'm probably going to come last," she added.

We all started saying how it was just for fun and it didn't matter who came where. Sally laughed and said, "Well, I was about to say that myself but you girls have said it for me. I've taught you everything you need to know. I might as well go home!"

Ricosha didn't realize she was joking and cried, "Oh no, don't! We need you!" and that made everyone else laugh too.

Sally also said we could do up our ponies for the cross country however we liked, as long as they were well groomed and tidy, and it didn't have to be all proper like the official Pony Club comps or anything. I got really creative on Charm and did a running plait in the mane with blue ribbons in, and gave him heart-shaped

quarter marks using a stencil
and some hairspray.

We all cleaned our
tack until it gleamed,
and then got into our
best gear. I'd saved my
cream jodhs especially
for the comp and
my pink stripy top
had least mud on it
so I wore that too, with
my body protector underneath. My pink silk
almost matches it, and with that and my long
boots on I felt like a proper cross-country rider!
I felt even more like one when Jody gave us
numbers to pin on to our tops. No one else
wanted to go last and I said I didn't mind, so I
was number 6!

Just as the parents started arriving, Sally
gathered us round in the yard and explained

the scoring system, which is like this:

First refusal – 4 penalty points

2nd refusal – 8 penalty points

3rd refusal – elimination

Knocking the gate down – 4 penalty points

Fall of pony – elimination

Fall of rider – 8 penalty points

2nd fall of rider – elimination.

I was so excited when our car pulled up and Mum and Dad and Hughie spilled out. Mum had told me she'd be coming on her own, so it was fab to see them all! Dad said, "A little bird gave us a call last night and said how well you were doing, so I took the day off work and we picked up Hughie on the way. We can't wait to see you in action, Charlie!" I gave them all hugs (even my smelly bro!). It was great seeing how proud they were of me before they'd even watched me ride one single step! And by the way, I found out later that the little bird was Sally!

When all the parents had arrived we mounted up and rode out to the field. I was feeling quite nervous, and Charm picked up on that and began prancing about, so I sat deep in my saddle, slowed my breathing down and relaxed through my shoulders and arms. It made me feel much better and Charm soon settled down too!

calm

After the warm-up and a practice jump each, it was time for the comp. The mums and dads, and Group A, and Lydia and Jody and James all leaned on the fence beside the ditch so that they could still see us when we jumped the hedge.

This is how we did:

Ricosha + Flame

Ricosha had a refusal at the log pile, so it wasn't a great start.

But she got it together and they flew round the rest of the course with no problems! *4 penalty points.*

Jemima + Mischief

Mischief ran out at the gate – twice! Jemima managed to get him over on the third try, so she didn't get eliminated, but she kept giggling, which didn't exactly help. And after the ditch Mischief did another lap round the field because he didn't want to stop! *12 penalty points!!*

Tameka + Shine

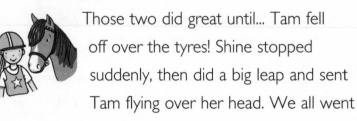

Those two did great until... Tam fell off over the tyres! Shine stopped suddenly, then did a big leap and sent Tam flying over her head. We all went

GASP! like we did when we were watching the Burghley DVD, but amazingly Tam was fine and she got back on and finished the course. Go, girl! *8 penalty points.*

Millie + Tally

Those two got eliminated for going the wrong way! Sally shouted out, "Millie, how many times have you done this course?" Millie was grinning, going, "I know, but it wasn't me who decided to race over to the other side of the field!" I don't think cheeky Tally's ever going to win her any prizes, but she loves him all the same! *Eliminated (whoops!).*

Skye + Fisher

Skye took it really slow and steady, going into trot between jumps, and if only they hadn't had the gate down, they would have gone clear. But it was very fragile! She got a bit flustered after that,

but we all cheered her on and she collected
her reins and trotted a circle round the tree
before taking off towards the tyre jump. Fisher
flew over that and the ditch, and when they
came to a stop Skye was absolutely beaming!
She kept saying she just couldn't believe
they'd jumped the whole course. Especially
when at the beginning of the week she never
even thought she'd come out here! *4 penalty
points (they did brilliantly!).*

And what about me?

Well, I wish I could write that
I had ZERO faults and I WON,
but that would be a BIG FIB!!

Charm went like a dream
over the log pile and we got
a lovely straight central approach over the
double. We turned quite late after that (my
fault – I was too busy thinking PHEW! about
us getting over the double without knocking

the second half down). Thank goodness the
hedge was next so we could brush through
it. If it had been the gate we'd definitely have
had it down. I pulled myself together then and
looked ahead, past the gate, and Charm just
got on and jumped it without me 'helping'
(ahem!).

Then we romped round
the tree in a balanced
canter, like the one we
had going on the beach
ride. We were nicely lined
up for the tyre jump, but
for some reason Charm put in
an extra stride at the last minute and jumped
a really long way over it, so we weren't
quite right for the ditch and he just suddenly
stopped in front of it.

The crowd at the fence all gasped as
I nearly went flying over his neck, but I

managed to hold on, just! My heart was pounding – we'd whizzed over the ditch in the morning lesson, so I just hadn't been expecting a refusal! But I shook off my disappointment and circled Charm round again.

Looking back now, I know what I did wrong on my second go, but I didn't realize it at the time. I tried to take charge and bobbed up too soon, just the thing Sally had warned me not to do! It unbalanced Charm and he clattered to a stop in front of the ditch again. One more refusal and we'd be eliminated.

I was about to get really frustrated but then I stopped myself. After all, me and Charm were a team and we weren't going to go to pieces at the last hurdle (and it actually was the last hurdle – hee hee!). I imagined us jumping the driftwood on the beach and tried to feel like I had felt then. The thought made me smile, and when I relaxed Charm did too.

♡ Charlie and Charm ♡

I trotted on, rode a circle and picked up canter as I turned in front of the tyre jump. I kept Charm really collected so we'd have lots of impulsion and he'd know that we could easily clear the ditch. I looked up and ahead like it was no big deal, gave Charm a final squeeze to urge him on ... and then we were landing. We were over! Instead of sitting forward too soon,

I'd just naturally left my seat and hinged at the hips at the right time without even thinking about it. I had felt like I was part of the movement. Like I was part of Charm!

So in the end I had 12 faults, the same as Jemima, meaning that we came joint last apart from Millie!!

Oh well, never mind!!

We all got rosettes, though, so I've still got something to put on my wall! Mum took pix of us all after the prize-giving, but I haven't printed them out yet so here's my drawing:

Ricosha Tameka me! Skye Jemima Millie

When Sally presented me with my rosette, Mum and Dad were clapping and cheering just as much as if I'd come first! I didn't really mind being second to last – especially because Jemima put her arm through mine and called out, "We're joint nearly last! Take a bow, Charlie!"

We both took a bow at the same time and everyone laughed and clapped for us. We were in fits of giggles and I said, "I can't believe it! I really thought you'd win!"

Jemima's eyes widened and she said, "Did you? I really thought you would!"

After we'd taken our ponies back to the barn and untacked them, we got drinks and watched Group A playing their gymkhana games. It was great fun clapping and cheering for them and when the last race came round I didn't want it to end! Soon it was time to bring our stuff downstairs. We went into the older girls' room to swap addresses, and all nine of us ended up piling together in a special Pony Camp hug! When Sally came up to see where we'd got to, we'd toppled over and were lying on the floor in total hysterics!

Skye held up her rosette and said to Sally, "I still can't believe it!"

Sally grinned. "You did it one step at a time, that's all it takes! Isn't that right, Charlie?"

I sat up and gave her a puzzled look.
I didn't know what she was talking about at
first. But then I realized she meant that I'd got
over Apple by just taking one step at a time.

Getting back on to a yard and joining in
with the girls was one step, and so was making
friends with Charm. Having a go at the cross
country was another step, and our teamwork
on the beach ride was a step too. And finally,
trusting each other to tackle that ditch was a
big step (well, a giant leap actually!).

It was so hard to say goodbye to the girls,
and even when we'd brought our stuff down
we kept hugging and taking photos and then
hugging more, until Ricosha's mum said
she really had to head off because it's
quite a way to Croydon. It was time to say
goodbye to the ponies then (boo hoo!).

I made a great big fuss of Charm, my
fabulous pony for the week, and told him how

wonderful he was. Also, I said sorry again for
being such a grouch at the start of Pony Camp
and whispered about 24 thank yous in his ear
for teaching me so much.

Of course, I'll never forget Apple,
but thanks to Charm I'm ready
to start riding some of the lovely
ponies at my stables. If I start
going to the lessons again I'll get to
hang around the yard and help out with the
other girls too. I might even enter our local
cross-country comp, because now I've had a
go at it I don't want to stop! I could ask to take
Flicka from the stables, or maybe my friend
Lucy would lend me her dapple grey, Storm.
And who knows, perhaps one day, if I'm lucky,
I'll even get another pony of my own!

So, thank you Sunnyside, and thank you
Charm!

Charlie xxx

PONY CAMP diaries

Learn all about
the world of ponies!

Glossary

Bending – directing the horse to ride correctly around a curve.

Bit – the piece of metal that goes inside the horse's mouth. Part of the bridle.

Chase Me Charlie – a show jumping game where the jumps get higher and higher.

Currycomb – a comb with rows of metal teeth used to clean (to curry) a pony's coat.

Dandy brush – a brush with hard bristles that removes the dirt, hair, and any other debris stirred up by the currycomb.

Frog – the triangular soft part on the underside of the horse's hoof. It's very important to clean around it with a hoof pick.

Girth – the band attached to the saddle and buckled around the horse's barrel to keep the saddle in place.

Grooming – the daily cleaning and caring for the horse to keep them healthy and make them beautiful for competitions. A full groom includes brushing your horse's coat, mane and tail and picking out the hooves.

Gymkhana – a fun event full of races and other competitions.

Hands – a way to measure the height of a horse.

Glossary

Mane – the long hair on the back of a horse's neck. Perfect for plaiting!

Manège – an enclosed training area for horses and their riders.

Numnah – a piece of material that lies under the saddle and stops it from rubbing against the horse's back.

Paces – a horse has four main paces, each made up of an evenly repeated sequence of steps. From slowest to quickest, these are the walk, trot, canter and gallop.

Plodder – a slow, reliable horse.

Pommel – the raised part at the front of the saddle.

Pony – a horse under 14.2 hands in height.

Rosette – a rose-shaped decoration with ribbons awarded as a prize! Usually, a certain colour matches the place you come in during the competition.

Stirrups – foot supports attached to the sides of a horse's saddle.

Tack – the main pieces of the horse's equipment, including the saddle and bridle. Tacking up a horse means getting them ready for riding.

ᔔ Pony Colours ᔕ

*Ponies come in all kinds of **colours**. These are some of the most common!*

Bay – Bay ponies have rich brown bodies and black manes, tails and legs.

Black – A true black pony will have no brown hairs and the black can be so pure that it looks a bit blue!

Chestnut – Chestnut ponies have reddish-brown coats that vary from light to dark red with no black points.

Dun – A dun pony has a sandy-coloured body, with a black mane, tail and legs.

Grey – Grey ponies come in a range of colour varieties, including dapple grey, steel grey, and rose grey.

Palomino – Palominos have a sandy-coloured body with a white or cream mane and tail. Their coats can range from pale yellow to bright gold!

Piebald – Piebald ponies have a mixture of black patches and white patches – like a cow!

Skewbald – Skewbald ponies have patches of white and brown.

৩ Pony Markings ৩

*As well as the main body colour, many ponies
also have white **markings** on their faces
and legs!*

On the legs:

Socks – run up above the fetlock but lower
than the knee. The fetlock is the joint above
the hoof.

Stockings – extend to at least the bottom of the
horse's knee, sometimes higher.

On the face:

Blaze – a wide, straight stripe down the face
from in between the eyes to the muzzle.
Snip – a white marking on the horse's
muzzle, between the nostrils.

Star – a white marking between the eyes.
Stripe – the same as a blaze but narrower.
White/bald face – a very wide blaze that
goes out past the eyes, making most of the
horse's face look white!

Fan-tack-stic Cleaning Tips!

*Get your **tack** shining in no time with these top tips!*

- Clean your tack after every use, if you can. Otherwise, make sure you at least rinse the bit under running water and wash off any mud or sweat from your girth after each ride.
- The main things you will need are:
  - bars of saddle soap
  - a soft cloth
  - a sponge
  - a bottle of leather conditioner
- As you clean your bit, check that it has no sharp edges and isn't too worn.
- Use a bridle hook or saddle horse to hold your bridle and saddle as you clean them. If you don't have a saddle horse, you can hang a blanket over a gate to put the saddle on. Avoid hanging your bridle on a single hook or nail because the leather might crack!

- Make sure you look carefully at the bridle before undoing it so that you know how to put it back together!
- Use the conditioner to polish the leather of the bridle and saddle and make them sparkle!
- Check under your numnah before you clean it. If the dirt isn't evenly spread on both sides, you might not be sitting evenly as you ride.
- Polish your metalwork occasionally. Cover the leather parts around it with a cloth and only polish the rings – not the mouthpiece, because that would taste horrible!

Going the Distance!

Find out how much you know about cross-country riding with this fun quiz! Can you go the distance?

1. For safety, the rider must wear:
   a. A body warmer
   b. A body protector
   c. Full body armor

2. Cross-country boots can be worn by your pony to:
   a. Look stylish
   b. Make them go faster
   c. Protect their legs from knocks

3. "Narrow," "angled," and "corner" are all types of:
   a. Events
   b. Fences
   c. Ditches

4. Cross-country riding differs from racing, as your pony should never finish:
   a. Exhausted
   b. Hungry
   c. Angry

5. Cross country forms part of three day eventing competitions, along with:

   a. Showjumping and racing

   b. Showjumping and dressage

   c. Dressage and dressing-up

6. A cross-country rider usually wears a:

   a. Skull cap

   b. Skeleton cap

   c. Shower cap

7. All cross-country courses are designed to:

   a. Look the same

   b. Look different

   c. Look exciting but a little scary

8. An advanced water combination includes a number of:

   a. Riders and routes

   b. Riders and fences

   c. Fences and routes

৶ Pretty Plaits! ৶

Follow this step-by-step guide to give your pony a perfect tail plait!

1. Start at the very top of the tail and take two thin bunches of hair from either side, plaiting them into a strand in the centre.

2. Continue to pull in bunches from either side and plait down the centre of the tail.

3. Keep plaiting like this, making sure you're pulling the hair tightly to keep the plait from unravelling!

4. When you reach the end of the dock – where the bone ends – stop taking in bunches from the side but keep plaiting downwards until you run out of hair.

5. Fasten with a plait band!

Gymkhana Ready!

Get your pony looking spectacular for the gymkhana with these grooming ideas!

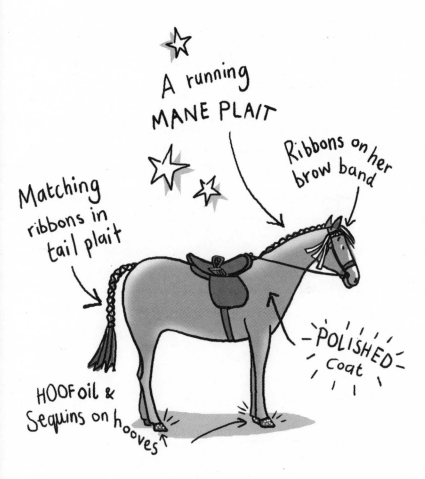

A running MANE PLAIT

Ribbons on her brow band

Matching ribbons in tail plait

POLISHED Coat

HOOF oil & Sequins on hooves

Turn the page for a sneak peek
at the next story in the series!

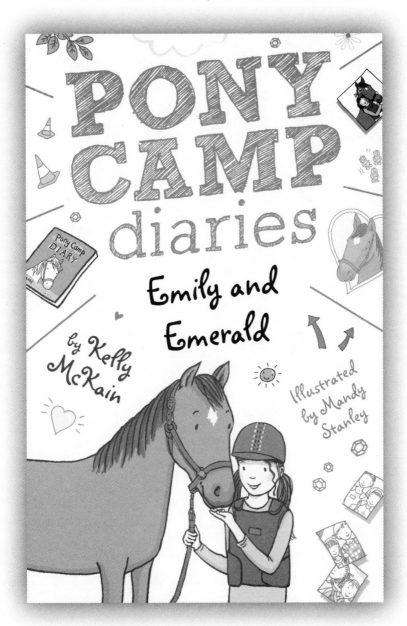

Monday - I can't believe I'm really here at Pony Camp!

I feel EXCITED about being here but NERVOUS at the same time!

I'm EXCITED 'cos I haven't ridden since we moved down here from London three weeks ago – I can't wait to get back in the saddle! And I'm NERVOUS because at the stables where I used to ride and help out at weekends there were these older girls and ... well, I don't really want to write all about what happened with them in my lovely new Pony Camp Diary. And, anyway, this is meant to be a new beginning.

Actually, me and Mum are both having a fresh start down here in Dorset. As it's the summer holidays I haven't started my new school yet, so it's been a bit boring 'cos I've just been helping Mum unpack boxes and paint the living room.

I felt extra NERVOUS when Jody showed us up here to my room. I wanted Mum to stay for a while, but she had to go back to the new house and wait for the gasman, so I ended up on my own. There are three beds in here, and Jody said the one by the window was her daughter Millie's, so I had the choice out of the bunk beds. I went for the bottom one, and as I started unpacking my stuff, I could hear all this noise and laughter coming from the room next door.

The two girls in there were really loud and confident – the exact opposite of ME! Then I heard all these footsteps on the stairs and someone yelling, "Hey, Harry!" at the top of their voice. For about one second I thought there was a BOY at Pony Camp, but then I heard this girl's voice yelling back and I realized that Harry must be short for Harriet.

And that was when Frankie bustled in with her mum, who is also really loud and who kept on calling her Francesca. I felt really shy and I wished I could shrink into a corner and disappear. But when Frankie rolled her eyes at me, I couldn't help smiling. She shooed her mum out and said hello, and after a few seconds of me blushing shyly with no words coming out I finally managed to mumble, "Hi, I'm Emily."

Frankie said, "Hi, Ems. Call me Frankie, everyone does. Well, apart from her, of course!"

She waved towards the door, obviously meaning her mum. "And my big sister Harry when she's trying to annoy me! That's her loud voice you can hear, by the way – she's got such a big mouth!"

I smiled as she threw her stuff on the top bunk. No one's ever called me Ems before – I quite like it. I was trying to think of something to say when Harry put her head round the door and shouted, "Come on, Frog Face, we're all going down to the yard!"

She grabbed Frankie's arm and started pulling her out of the room. Frankie giggled and cried, "Don't call me Frog Face, Monkey Breath!" Then Frankie tried to grab my arm, and I wanted to go with them, but my feet stayed stuck to the spot. For some reason, I don't seem to be that good at joining in.

"I'll be down in a sec!" I told them as brightly as I could. "I just want to start off my diary first."

So that's what I've been doing!

Oh, hang on, even the other room with the younger girls in has gone quiet so everyone must be outside. Right, I'm going to take a deep breath and put on my hat and body protector (and a big smile), and go down to the yard.

Monday 1.45p.m. - well, I still can't believe what happened this morning!

I'm so EXCITED and NERVOUS again! EXCITED because I have met the most amazing pony called Emerald, who I'm desperate to have as my own for the week. And NERVOUS because I'm waiting to hear from Sally, our instructor, about whether I can have her or not.

Sally's gone off to speak to Johnny about it (he's the yard manager and also Millie's dad), and she said she'll come and find me after lunch. We've finished eating now, and I'm writing this sitting at the picnic table outside the farmhouse so I can keep a lookout for her.

OK, well, this is a pic of (fingers crossed!) my fab pony, Emerald!

Emerald

She isn't supposed to be one of the Pony Camp ponies at all, but as soon as I saw her I knew I wanted her, and Sally did admit it seems like Emerald has chosen me too. But she also said I'd have to ride Flame first in the assessment and, oh whoops, I'm trying to say everything at once and missing things out. Right, I'll take a deep breath and slow down and write everything in order.

OK, so I headed over to the yard to find the others, and as I walked between the car park and lower field this pony came bolting towards me, completely loose, with a head collar on

and her lead rope dangling. It was Emerald!
I didn't know her name then, of course. And I
didn't know that she'd just arrived at Sunnyside
and had gone bombing out of the trailer as Sally
was unloading her. But I did know that she was
the most gorgeous pony I'd ever seen.

She was skittering around, looking ever so
frightened. For a moment I froze in shock, but
then I thought how dangerous that dangling
lead rope was, and how I had to stop her from
tripping up and having an accident.

I stood my ground as she came right up
to me, and I spread my arms out so that she
couldn't get past and gallop off up the track to
the upper fields.

I took a deep breath and tried to relax.
Emerald lowered her head and snorted –
she seemed to be calming down a bit too. I
stepped towards her and put my hand out for
her to smell.

"Be careful!" Sally called as she appeared
round the corner. I gave a slight nod, then slowly
turned so I was standing at Emerald's shoulder,
and reached down for the end of the lead rope.

Then I stood there with both hands on the rope while Sally came over and took it from me. "Well done!" she said softly. "You showed a lot of horse sense by staying so calm."

I smiled, and inside I was really proud of myself.

She asked my name, and just when I thought she was going to send me off to the yard to join the others she said I could help take Emerald into the barn instead. She told me to lead her into a small pen in the corner, away from the other ponies. As I walked her on, I kept glancing at her gorgeous, glossy bay coat and cute white star and big brown eyes, and thinking how beautiful and special she was.

We got some hay for her and filled up her water trough, and as I was stroking her nose to say goodbye, I blurted out to Sally, "Do you think, maybe, I could have Emerald as my pony this week?"

Sally frowned. "I'm sorry, Emily, but she's not going to be ridden at Pony Camp for a while," she said. "She's very nervous and I need to work with her myself first."

I tried to smile but I couldn't hide how disappointed I was. Emerald leaned her head over the railing and nudged my arm. I rubbed her neck and she snorted gently.

"It wouldn't be an easy week," Sally said then. I stared at her. Was she saying yes after all? "I've ridden Emerald myself and I know her temperament and capabilities," she continued. "You won't be able to jump her, and you'll have to keep her calm in flat work or she might bolt off with you."

"I don't mind," I insisted. "I don't care about any of that, I just want to be with Emerald."

Sally smiled. "I know you do, Emily, but we have to be sensible. I'll need you to ride another pony in the assessment lesson, so I can see what level you're at. And then we'll think about it. OK?"

"OK!" I cried, grinning.

So I gave Emerald a last pat, and showed her that I had my fingers crossed for us. Then Sally and I went to join the others, who were all hanging around outside the office, squished on to the bench and chatting away. I hung back behind Sally as we neared them. I wish I could just talk to new people like that, as if I've known them for ages. Frankie and the others make it look so easy.

Everyone had already introduced themselves,
but Sally got them to say their names to me
too, which made me the centre of attention
and left me feeling completely embarrassed!

The other girls are:

Frankie   Morgan   Harriet   Neema   Elena   Madison   Chantelle   Millie

Harriet said she and Chantelle and Elena
(she's Spanish so you say it as Elay-na) are all 12
and in the same class at school. They're sharing
a room in the farmhouse too. Madison and
Morgan are 8 and 9, and they've come all the

way over from New York. They're staying with their English grandma for the summer, and she had the idea of sending them to Pony Camp. I just love their American accents! They're sharing the other room with Neema, who's only-just-9. Me and Frankie are both 10-nearly-11 so our room is the middly-aged one, which we're sharing with Millie.

The girls all seemed really nice, and as Sally read out the 'Safety on the Yard' rules I wished I could just pile on to the bench too, but I stayed put. I didn't quite dare join in with everyone, in case one of them shoved me off. Maybe that sounds a bit of a strange thing to say, but the older girls at my last yard seemed nice at first too, and they turned out to be really horrible, so I can't help thinking that kind of stuff.

Luckily, everyone had to get up then 'cos we were going on a tour around Sunnyside.

We found out about the fire drill meeting points, and we were learning the safety stuff as we went round – like in the tack room Sally told us that we must put any brushes or numnahs and things away after using them, and in the yard she showed us how to tie up a pony safely.

As we walked around, everyone was chattering together in a big group, so I just smiled and tried to join in here and there. When Sally showed us the barn everyone went completely crazy over the ponies that were being tacked up for us. But I was just gazing at Emerald, who was standing in her little pen, looking back at me.

Then it was time to get matched up with our ponies. Back in the yard, everyone started to pull on their hats and gloves, chatting excitedly. Sally got her list and read out who was on who, as Jody and Lydia, the stable girl, led the ponies out.

This is who everyone got:

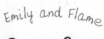
Emily and Flame

Chantelle and Charm

Elena and Jewel

Just for the assessment. Flame's beautiful but I really want Emerald!

Frankie and Star

Madison and Sugar

Morgan and Monsoon

Harriet and Shine

Millie and Tally (her own pony!)

Neema and Prince

Kelly McKain

Kelly McKain is a best-selling children's and YA author with more than 40 books published in more than 20 languages. She lives in the beautiful Surrey Heath area of the UK with her family and loves horses, dancing, yoga, singing, walking, and being in nature. She came up with the idea for the Pony Camp Diaries while she was helping young riders at a summer camp, just like the one at Sunnyside Stables! She enjoys hanging out at the Holistic Horse and Pony Center, where she plays with and rides cute Smartie and practices her natural horsemanship skills with the Quantum Savvy group. Her dream is to do some bareback, bridleless jumping like New Zealand Free Riding ace Alycia Burton, but she has a ways to go yet!